Harrowed Earth - Book Two

Cicero Wants You

Aaron Conaway

A K&Q Press Publication

Front Cover Art Credit: **Jeremy Bohannon**

"Harrowed Earth" logo created by **Jeremy Bohannon**

First Edition 2023

Books by Aaron Conaway

Harrowed Earth

Book 1 *Appalachian Blues*

Book 2 *Cicero Wants You*

The Timberhaven Chronicles

Waking the Weaver

Before the Weaver

Monsters in the Park (Coming Soon!)

The Michael Gideon Collection

Tales for Halloween

Tales for Halloween Vol. II

Table of Contents

Page 5   - The Way of the World: Part Two

Page 9   - Cicero Wants You!

Page 17 - The Myth of Coin: Preamble

Page 24 - Banesska's Traveling Game

Page 50 - The Myth of Coin: The Coronation

Page 61 - A Digger's Woe

Page 86 - The Myth of Coin: Dark Deeds

Page 141 - Epilogue

Page 155 - Explore More of the World of Harrowed
Earth

The Way of the World: Part Two

Earth.

Human population living planetside Pre-Worldfall: roughly 700 million worldwide.

Human population living planetside Post-Worldfall: unknown.

Human population in The Kingdom: seventy-one thousand souls, not including transients or visiting merchants.

The Kingdom. Eight hundred and twenty-eight square kilometers that had once been Kansas City and its various suburbs are now a collection of seventeen individually-gated baronies.

Life in The Kingdom is the closest thing to a Pre-Worldfall existence that its citizens have found. Countless villages, even some towns, are scattered

5

throughout the nearly fifteen hundred kilometers

between The Kingdom and the boundaries of the

Unknown Land. Still, the peak of civilization lies to

the west of The Wastes, behind the walls of The

Kingdom.

It's anyone's guess why the alien overlords,

the Ravok-Dyn, don't raze The Kingdom to the

ground from the safety of their city-ships. However,

some think the proximity to the warzone of The

Shift—a star-filled abyss of folded space that once

was the Pacific Ocean—allows humanity their

refuge.

Only time will tell.

Humanity tries to forge a new destiny in

alien-brought darkness, taking meager steps toward

a future that keeps trying to kill them.

Yet watch as they find their way.

Bards: Bards serve as peacekeepers, lawmakers, historians, and beyond. They recruit new bodies into their fold through storytelling and other entertaining activities. Scarves and sashes of various lengths and colors denote a bard. Most also carry a walking staff, spear, or bullwhip.

Technolomists: Technolomists do their best to mend broken people in a ravaged world, utilizing healing technology, teachings, and powers learned over the ages. Their practices and abilities are some of the only evidence left on Earth of pre-Ravok-Dyn's arrival. Though the severe distrust of higher technology is rampant, most schooled in

Technolomistry hail from bloodlines where healing

powers are still active.

Cicero Wants You!

The Barony of Tuggett's Knee

Northeast of Edwardsville, Kansas PW (Pre-

Worldfall)

(Fifteen hours before the Coronation)

"A lot of you here only remember living

under a dark green sky," Cicero began, her long,

black hair braid wrapped around her left arm. A red

sash hung from her waist, indicating her standing as

a bard. Her smooth voice was steady. Then, needing

the young adults gathered under the big tent to hear

her, Cicero began weaving her tale as she walked in

slow circles before them. "You don't recall a sky of

blue or storm clouds without the red-tinged promise of imminent death glowing within them."

One in her audience, a pale, dark-haired girl, flinched at this. *Good*, Cicero thought. *I'm getting their attention.*

"2006. When our planet, the world Earth, began changing irrevocably." Cicero continued, her eyes scanning the small crowd. "I was only fourteen, the same age as some here. And while, yes, we'd seen humanity changed with the advent of the superpowered some ten years before, Mother Earth was still Home.

"But then the Otherworlders came."

Cicero stopped circling, standing silently to signify that her tale was about to change. Marrying physicality, voice fluctuations, and timed gestures to a bard's tale had been part of Cicero's base training.

Simple teachings, compared to the intense scrutiny

of one's tale-telling ability in later lessons. But a

bard's function was important in this world of 2026.

They served as entertainment, true (Cicero had just

finished her famous reimagining of the old world

classic *Indiana Jones and the Temple of Ark*). Still,

bards were also this age's teachers—its historians.

They were the clinging hope that humanity could

know where it'd been to rediscover where it was

going—last vestiges, the kindling spark that people

could do more than merely survive.

For that, though, the Guild needed fresh

faces, new recruits. But the human population was

guessed at being only 140 million on Earth (all

communication with the rest of the planet—not to

mention people off-world—was impossible due to the Otherworlders' takeover), and a bard's life was dangerous. They traveled desolate roads across meager lands filled with more things to do them harm than not, all in a quest for rumored villages and occasionally serving as peacekeepers whenever they found those villages. As such, all bards trained in various fighting techniques, munitions, and combat anatomy. (A more subtle way of describing they knew where to strike to kill things, be those things foreign or domestic.)

These were reasons parents didn't clamor for their children to hear sales pitches like the one Cicero was spinning, though few kept their kids from listening when a night under the big tent presented itself. But bards were forbidden to ask any outright to join their ranks. So, what couldn't be asked for needed to be obtained through art.

"In the days before, we had movies. They were living pictures that told a story." Cicero explained. "In those movies, humanity would forget its hatred of each other, band together in a breathtaking display of unity, and defeat the aliens. In some movies, it took a war with the invaders: in others, a well-placed trick or explosion.

"In reality, the Otherworlders had been claiming our planet for decades with secret plans and back-alley deals. As a result, we native people of Earth had lost our home before we knew we should be fighting for it."

Cicero rounded back to the pale girl. She was sitting with two friends—a boy and another girl, engaged by Cicero's tale but only hearing it. The pale girl was *listening*.

"So now, some ten years since the world fell —of living amidst the broken squalor of defeat by circumstance—I stand before you telling my bard's tales. Making a stalwart oath that this life can be more than monsters and disease, richer than gnawing hunger and unsettling dreams. You look to our horizon now and see only Otherworlders' floating metropolises, the mechanized wall of alien dominance. I would have you see blue skies again and know that we are all of us capable of more than we think."

There was sometimes thunderous applause after Cicero's pitch. Occasionally, stunned silence mixed with tears. This time, however, the crowd of young teens seemed galvanized. Dare Cicero to

think it; they seemed eager to wear the sash.

"Okay, children," a skinny man opened the

tent flaps with a flourish of anger. Someone's

parent, Cicero assumed. "The show is over. Thank

the bard on your way out. Forget not that Tuggett

Knee's curfew is in ten minutes, so let's all find our

ways home, shall we?"

The children emptied their seats and began

to file out of the tent, some congratulating Cicero

for an excellent evening as they went. Finally

unwrapping her long braid from her arm and

gathering the ropes needed to help break down the

bard's tent, Cicero looked up to see the pale girl,

sans friends, standing before her. Cicero offered a

gentle smile to the awkward girl. It seemed she *had* been listening.

"My name's Sepia," the girl offered shyly, "Sepia de Winter. I wondered if I might ask you some questions—about how to become a bard."

The Myth of Coin: Preamble

The Barony of Tuggett's Knee

The Temple

West of Washington Square Park

Kansas City, MO PW

(Pre-Worldfall)

(Thirty minutes before the Coronation)

Smoke hung throughout the low-lit room as

the men inside waited for word to begin their work.

They were diligent in their mindfulness of the job at

hand; were these shadows, these hellbent strangers

—tightly coiled springs awaiting release.

Like hounds before the hunt, they just

needed the signal.

* * * * *

Philip turned his cufflinks as he looked in the mirror so that the letter *K*—the initial of his last name—was upright. He always did so unthinkingly while wearing them, but Philip never noticed, his mindset being ever above his current station. He walked to the nightstand and retrieved a thin dagger, stashing it in his boot, something his father had taught him when Philip was a boy. The blade was long enough to kill but short enough to miss his ankle bone while hidden away.

"For the bindings, if you're ever caught and tied up," Philip's father had said. "Though, if your hands are bound behind your back, that'll be a different fish to fry."

His father had been a fool when it came to turns of phrases, but Philip had always come out the better for having a knife on hand. He couldn't deny the results.

"Ready, sire?" Renault asked from the door. Philip thought Renault's gray wig, an evident sign of his station, never looked askew or out of place on the man's head.

"I am," Philip said, standing upright. He pulled the front of his suit jacket down sharply, causing the tails at the back of the coat to fly up in aggravation before resting along the backs of his legs.

"Today is the day, sir," Renault said, beaming. "Your parents would be so proud."

"Let's not oversell it, Renault," Philip said as he walked past the man and into the hall. "My parents sold tractor tires to desperate farm folk in middle America. They wouldn't understand the first thing about my ambition, my plans. Come now, time to be done with this pageantry."

Philip couldn't help but walk a little straighter, though, his shoulders pulling back as he made his way down the hall. Renault bowed and followed closely after.

The world his parents had known was long gone, swallowed in the changing status quo. Philip had grown up rich—well, wealthy so far as flyover states were concerned. Money had always provided, in all things and all ways, for his family. It kept the world spinning, built into the structure of everything, before the fall.

But, as everyone learned some ten years ago, none of that safety or structure had been real. Society was a lie, built on a house of cards, and those with actual power had blown it all down, showing everyone on Earth the truth behind the lie. Whether the so-called superheroes of the day or the Ravok-Dyn had been to blame never mattered.

The world fell.

Power made that happen, not money.

Those in The Kingdom were attempting to rebuild a society that had already failed them, propping the lie up in fantasy dress and playacting.

Philip would play along.

For now.

They were holding his coronation in The Temple—once known as Union Station in the world before—so everyone who was anyone in The Kingdom would be in attendance. But, of course, it wasn't every day that a new baron rose, The Quorum proclaiming fresh council among The Kingdom's baronies.

Philip stopped as the hall opened into a vast room, looking down from his perch as people began filling the chamber. A hundred lit lanterns filled the space, mimicking the sun-filled days of Earth-That-Was. *This is it*, he told himself, watching as dozens of people milled about, making pleasantries as they found their seats, all waiting for him to arrive. *The start of everything I've dreamed of—a mere first*

step of many.

Banesska's Traveling Game

The Barony of Tuggett's Knee

(Fourteen hours before the Coronation)

Two teens exited the bard's large tent onto dust-covered, crumbling asphalt. It had once been a city street in another lifetime. A slight wind caught up the dirt, pitching it around as the friends walked with the twitchy energy that comes from being young and unchaperoned.

"How can you say that?" the dark-skinned teen, Kendra, asked, unrolling the sleeves of her flannel shirt in a futile effort to keep out the dirt, "Indiana Jones could've been a woman. There's so much we don't know!"

"Because," her conversational sparring partner, a boy named Wade, announced, "my cousin lives down south, in a village off old Interstate 44? And he said that there's some grandpa there, sells pre-Shift collectibles from a cave, who has a, uh–"

"A poster," offered a third girl, Sepia, her pale arm draped through the crook in Wade's deep brown one as she caught up with her friends.

"Right, it was a poster! And it says *Indiana Jones* at the top of it. Bullwhip, hat, everything Cicero described in her story tonight; only he's a guy."

"Whatever," Kendra huffed as the trio turned down another decrepit road toward the big wooden fence that separated Tuggett's Knee, the barony where Kingdom-famous Cicero had just performed antique stories to a crowd under her big

tent, from Sepia's home barony of Renaissance.

Sepia laid her head on Wade's shoulder as

they walked, her pale skin, the tell-tale sign of her

de Winter blood, flushed by the battle between cold

night air and her hormones.

"What do you say we go back and ask

Cicero," Kendra asked, trying not to feel like an

awkward third wheel and kicking a stone as she

failed, "find out once and for all?"

"Yeah, like Sepia's going to stay out any

later and risk getting busted," Wade tickled Sepia

under her arm, smiling, "She's too scared of

disappointing her uncle."

Sepia wriggled away from Wade with a

laugh; he still had the long, black wrap she was

wearing caught up in his hands. She half-heartedly

hid behind Kendra, who had stopped still.

"Speaking of, where'd you run off to after

the show?" Kendra asked Sepia, trying not to smile

at Wade's jibe.

"Oh, I, uh, I dropped this," Sepia fumbled,

freeing her wrap from Wade. "And had to double

back. But anyhow, *you're* one to talk, Wade

Batalon. Mr. 'I can't hang out because I've got an

important job.'" Sepia mimicked Wade's deeper

voice.

"You forgot 'I'm the youngest digger ever,'"

Kendra added, doing her own impression.

"And you, Ms. Lawden," Sepia continued,

turning on Kendra. "Don't think I missed that

smirk. Studying to become a technolomist is *huge*.

I'm not the only one here worried about disappointing someone."

"That's supposed to be me?" Wade asked, feigning offense. "You two should join Banneska's and hit the road."

All three laughed, walking Sepia toward her home barony until she pulled them both back short, stopping in the road.

"I don't want to go home yet," Sepia admitted. "How often *are* the three of us free at the same time? So let's stay out!"

"We could go *hit* Banneska's," Kendra said as she began to smile. Suddenly, she wanted the night to continue as well. "Maybe catch the last Battle Board?"

"Oh, you *know* I'm in!" Wade grinned. "No betting, though. Collecting a claim this late takes forever, and I've got an early shift tomorrow."

Kendra and Sepia looked at each other for a beat before yelling in booming voices, *"I'm the youngest digger ever!"*

* * * * *

Banesska's Traveling Game was a wayfaring carnival like the wandering fairs of old. It was home to some fifty people—performers, artists, athletes, and laborers—composed of souls who couldn't abide roots even after an apocalypse. The famed C.G. Banesska assembled the outfit and ran things as they roamed a cultivated circuit throughout the Known Lands. Tuggett's Knee was one of the largest baronies in The Kingdom, so Banesska's

Traveling Game always set up shop there when it traveled through, much to the dismay of some of the other baronies.

One could find all manner of adventures under the tents at Banesska's. Treasures undreamt of, too. But for real excitement (and tidy profits, if one were so inclined to bet on matches), the discerning visitor sought the game that Banesska built the entire show around—Battle Board.

The Battle Board consisted of a square vertical wall nine meters tall by nine meters wide. One side of the wall was painted blue, while the other was green. Eight, three-meter cylindrical metal poles were placed equidistant through the wall in a perfect 9x9 grid, minus the center of the wall, which contained a circular hole of empty air.

"So it's always one on one?" Sepia asked as the trio made their way through the milling crowd.

"Not always," Kendra explained. "Two on two is common, and even three on three is not unheard of."

"But one-to-one is the best," Wade grinned. "It can get *crazy*."

"Oh, man!" Kendra beamed, looking at the large, handwritten sign listing the upcoming tournaments and each participant's odds of winning. "Dart is about to go up!"

"Don't get too excited," Wade said, shaking his head. He pointed toward where a man in blue and green coveralls was updating the listing. "Dart's going against The Kraken. 50 to 1 odds of winning."

"I'd take that bet," Kendra said. "If we *were* betting."

"Why such terrible odds?" Sepia asked, looking at all the people starting to surround the event.

"Well, The Kraken *is* huge," Kendra began. "With a higher win percentage. Dude can do *massive* damage if he gets a piece of you. But Dart's smaller mass makes her faster on the 'ports."

"The teleporting I get," Sepia said. "That's what the poles allow for, players in a costume—"

"Rigs," Kendra interrupted. "They're rigs, not costumes."

"Oh, come on!" Sepia laughed. "Dart's dressed in blue camouflage tactical wear, and her motorcycle helmet is sporting little wings. That's in line with a pre-Worldfall crimefighting costume, or I've never read a history DOC file."

"Regardless," Wade added, nodding at Kendra. "She's right."

"Fine *rigs*," Sepia continued. "The rigs allow them to both maintain the perpendicular gravity of the wall and bounce around within the corral of the poles."

"Exactly. So what *don't* you get?" Kendra asked as the trio moved closer.

"How one wins a match is where I'm iffy," Sepia admitted.

"I'd like to take this one," Wade interjected. "If I may, Cap'n?"

"Floor is yours, Cap'n." Kendra mock

bowed and rolled her hand in a "please, continue"

gesture.

Sepia rolled her eyes. "Hey, I think I'm

doing pretty well here for never having seen a

match before!"

"Indeed, young student," Wade smiled. "But

as the game is about to start, let me speed us along.

As the teens watched, more people swam

around the Battle Board. This was the night's big

event, and everyone wanted to watch the action.

Then Kendra noticed something that

distracted her from the Battle Board frenzy. Magena

Bedard, Baroness of Tuggett's Knee, dressed in a

plain, off-white robe, was quietly making her way

up the slender staircase of a tented pavilion standing ten meters above them.

And there, leaning on its balcony, was the man himself: C.G. Banesska.

*   *   *   *   *

"Your honeyed wine, sir," a bald, spindly young man in burnt orange robes handed a sphere-shaped glass to a dark-skinned man dressed in a luscious deep purple tunic. The older man had been stroking his gray goatee, deep in thought.

"This close to Renaissance, I believed *mead* to be the preferred nomenclature," the man smiled, taking the glass.

"Of course, sir," the younger man averted his eyes toward the floor. "My apologies. Your mead."

"There's no need to fuss over it," the man smiled, sitting the glass on a nearby table and returning his view toward the Battle Board. "That will be all."

"I am here, C.G.," a woman's voice came from outside the tent.

The young man in the robes disappeared at her arrival as C.G. turned to the sound of her voice.

"Baroness," C.G. said with a big smile. "You honor my tent."

"At three stories tall, it's hardly a tent," the short, brown-skinned woman said, returning his smile. "And it's just us here, Charles. It's Maggie."

The pair embraced, and when parting, C.G.

said with a laugh, "Maggie, my friend. It is so good

to find you well. At least, I trust that's how I've

found you?"

"Now that Cicero is here, yes," Magena

said, sighing in relief as she did so. "Thank you for

altering your performance schedule for us."

"Make no mistake, my friend," C.G. said,

raising his glass. "I adore you, but the circuit is a

harsh mistress. It was Cicero who moved mountains

to be here when you called." He swigged his drink.

"All thanks should go to her. In fact—"

C.G.'s eyes bulged as his throat began to

close. He dropped the glass to the floor, shattering it

upon impact, and fell to his knees, gasping for air

that would not come.

"Charles!" Magena screamed. A young blonde woman in burnt orange robes ran in. She stifled a cry as she took in the scene.

"Run, find a technolomist," Magena ordered. "Hurry!"

*   *   *   *   *

"So, the rigs are shells, yeah?" Wade continued. "Kind of like teched-out suits of armor from Cicero's antique stories. Now, a player can dress their rig up however they like, they're all the same template underneath, but they're stuck picking from only one of three sizes: the small ones—like Dart uses—are called Daggers. They're tiny but can still do the job. Large rigs, i.e., The Kraken, we call that rig a Hammer."

"The midsize rig is a Flail," Kendra chimed in. "No one knows why."

"*To win the match*," Wade said, flaring his eyes wide at Kendra, "a player has to ground their opponent."

"But how is that possible," Sepia asked, turning her head sideways as she looked at the Battle Board. "If the suits allow them to defy gravity and run at a horizontal angle?"

The trio stopped moving through the crowd as Kendra sat them at a makeshift set of bleachers beneath what she now knew to be C.G. Banesska's very own pavilion.

"This would go faster if I could finish!"

Wade huffed as each girl caught the other smiling.

"I'm sorry," Sepia said. "Pray, continue."

she curtsied.

"There's only enough juice to power rigs for

five minutes. No power means no more defying

gravity. Now, that's five minutes if a player stands

up there and does nothing. But that's not Battle

Board. Porting takes from that power bank.

Running. Fighting.

"Plus, there are two ways a rig goes

completely dead besides running out of juice,"

Kendra said. "What? You were taking too long. The

match is about to start!" she pointed to the betting

windows closing as Wade sighed.

"If a player takes too many hits, too much damage," Kendra returned to Sepia, "the rig shuts down. They're designed to let a player fall from that nine-meter wall unscathed, so it translates that damage, tricking the rig into thinking it fell. It tucks the combatant into a nice medical cocoon, and the match ends."

"Finally, if a player gets out of range of the pillars' net," Kendra pointed to the metal pillars in the Battle Board, "by hopping over the top or around the sides of the wall rather than porting—"

Magena Bedard's scream could be heard, even over the noise of the growing crowd. Kendra looked up to where she knew the baroness to be, so she saw, seconds later, a robed girl come from the stairs yelling something.

"A technolomist," Sepia yelled, piecing the girl's shouts together. "Kendra, go!"

* * * * *

"I don't have a kit, any tech," Kendra's voice shook as she knelt over the body of C.G. Banesska, his eyes rolling back in his skull. Yellow froth formed at his mouth as he managed slight, pained wheezes.

"You must do what you can, Kendra," Magena spoke softly, yet it was still the firmest voice Kendra had ever heard. "More help is coming, but he's too far gone."

Kendra felt his throat for any obstructions but immediately chided herself. *Fool! This looks like a reaction to something toxic. I could properly*

assess him if I had time to—

"Wait," Kendra interrupted her own thought

process. "A rig. Get me a rig from Battle Board!"

"Kendra, we're losing him!" Magena

grabbed the girl by the shoulders.

But Wade and Sepia had already begun

doing what their friend had ordered.

"Where are the rigs stored?" Wade asked the

robed girl.

"I-in the base of the pavilion," she said.

Then, realizing she could help her benefactor,

"Follow me!"

Kendra shook loose of Magena and knelt

back to her patient.

"I have a plan," Kendra spoke loudly to the dying man and the newly-filled room of people who had seemingly appeared only to watch a tragedy unfold. She placed both hands on either side of Banesska's head, stilling it while carefully avoiding the sputum, as his body began to contort and shake, his feet kicking.

Magena made to push her out of the way.

"Kendra, what are you—"

"Don't!" Kendra yelled with a force she didn't recognize in her own voice. "If you want to help, hold his shoulders, or these convulsions will damage his spine. Where is that rig!"

Magena did as the technolomist instructed.

"I hope a Flail will work," Wade called out as he and Sepia brought the Battle Board rig inside, pushing people out of the way as they came.

"Move, move!" Kendra shouted, willing the crowd to part. She let go of Banesska long enough to take the halo of the rig from Wade, then slipped it over her patient's head. "Put the boots, bracers, and chest plate on him. Hurry!"

Once the gear was in place, Kendra pushed the button on the halo at Banesska's temple, immediately enveloping him in a blue and gold suit of armor, seemingly of ancient Aztec design.

"Now," Kendra said, wiping sweat from her brow. "Let's throw him over the balcony."

* * * * *

The following morning, Kendra's mother had woken her with word that Baroness Bedard had sent for Kendra to meet her at the clinic at Kendra's earliest convenience.

"You've slept in terribly late," her mother said, "but that's okay, given the night you had. Still, best not to keep the Baroness waiting."

Her mother's advice aside, Kendra answered Magena Bedard's summons with a heavy foot that belied her typical nature. She changed from her sleeping clothes at a snail's pace and ate breakfast slowly. Finally, with nothing else to tarry her, Kendra made for the clinic where they'd taken the venerable C.G. Banesska after the attempt on his life.

I must have made a mistake, Kendra thought

over and over again. *I panicked and thought the*

rig's medical cocoon would—

"Ah, you're here," Magena said. Her hair

was unkempt, and bags were forming under her

eyes, but she was smiling.

Kendra felt her face warm in

embarrassment, having walked into the clinic

without minding where she was.

"Yes, ma'am," Kendra said quietly.

"This is my savior, then?" a deep voice

Kendra recognized from Battle Board matches

bellowed from behind Magena.

"Indeed," Magena replied, turning around.

"C.G. Banesska, may I introduce up-and-coming

technolomist Kendra Lawden."

Kendra walked around the Baroness and

went to the sickbed of her patient from the previous

night.

"It's an honor to formally meet you, sir,"

Kendra began, offering her hand out to shake.

"The honor, dear sage," C.G. held Kendra's

hand warmly, "is mine. I owe you my life, as I hear

it. I am entirely in your debt."

"I'm happy I was there to help," Kendra

beamed, unable to control herself. To settle her

emotions, she looked at the datatab of Mr.

Banesska's healing bed. Noticing something, she

squinted more closely and typed some info into the

datatab.

"What is it?" C.G. asked. "You look

puzzled."

"Well, it's probably nothing," Kendra began.

"No, go ahead," Magena said, touching Kendra's shoulder.

"Well, it's just that your vitals are weak, sure," Kendra explained. "That's to be expected. But the toxin in your bloodstream it's capsaicin-based."

"I'm sorry," C.G. said. "What does that mean?"

"It's," Kendra briefly went into her thoughts, puzzling at a medical dilemma like she was in a Technolomistry class. "Um, I mean, it's temporary. The poison. What they used to call an incapacitating agent pre-world fall. It means I don't think someone was trying to kill you after all."

The Myth of Coin: The Coronation

The Barony of Tuggett's Knee

The Temple

As she walked among the scores of people,

Cicero worried her fingers along the long red bard

sash hanging around her waist. A nervous tick she'd

picked up as a girl and had never quite outgrown.

Cicero hated events such as these, even if

she could see their *limited* usefulness. The

maneuverings of the rich and powerful played out in

full view of each other upon a revolving stage.

Also known as politics.

Cicero could feel eyes dart across her as she

moved about the room. She knew a bard in

attendance was quite a coup in these sorts of games, but it didn't make the staring any less annoying.

Cicero tried to focus on the music of the small band of minstrels hired for the coronation instead of the onlookers, let her eyes unfocus on the trees to better mind the forest, as it were. After all, she had an investigation to continue in exchange for Baroness Bedard having allowed Cicero to hold her recruitment drive with fewer chaperones last night.

Okay, Magena, Cicero thought, her eyes bouncing around the hall in time to the music filling it. *If you've got the game of cat and mice that you fear you do, let's see if I can narrow down your cast of players.*

The opulence of the wealthy changed after the world fell. One might think such an event could transform the survivors, but base humanity seemed to prefer seeking riches and the privilege they brought. Instead of flashy cars and jewelry, one's wallet and prestige are showcased with brightly colored robes.

The hall was quickly filling with a myriad of colors.

There were seventeen baronies in The Kingdom, so The Quorum meeting would suggest that nine leaders would be in attendance, but, luckily, that was not the case. While any of The Kingdom's barons or baronesses could join something so significant as this coronation, of course, The Quorum typically only consisted of leaders from the four biggest: Wayland de Winter,

Desmond Traiste, Rance Dibbek, and the person

that brought Cicero to the party, Magena Bedard.

Cicero eased her way around the crowd,

nodding greetings here and there to the few souls

who did more than whisper as she passed. Suddenly,

there was another person's arm in the crook of hers.

"My dear," Wayland de Winter said with a

smile as they continued to walk, "you don't appear

to be having a bit of fun at our little gala."

"Baron de Winter," Cicero curtly nodded to

the middle-aged, dirty blond-haired lord.

"Please, it's Wayland." his smile diminished

just enough to stop reaching his eyes. "I love my

brother, but the de Winter nonsense is all Horatio."

"Speaking of," Cicero stopped them

walking. "I spoke with Horatio's daughter, Sepia,

last evening. She's grown. I didn't recognize her at first."

"And how is my niece?"

"Interested in what I do." Cicero watched closely for any reaction, but the baron had a fantastic poker face.

"Well, won't her father be excited at the news," Wayland's smile once again reached his eyes. "Maybe it will take the sting out of the word we got this morning about the tragedy at the new Digger site."

"Yes," Cicero said. "I'd heard. That's awful. Do they know what happened?"

"We haven't gotten any new information yet. My, but this is a dreary conversational topic! Not at all what I came over for."

"How can I help you, Baron," Cicero asked. "I had hoped to greet a few other folks before the festivity begins."

"Of course," Wayland said. He started them moving around the hall again. "I just wondered what, if anything, you'd discovered about our *homme de l'heure,* this Prince of Torts?"

Cicero misstepped, but Wayland caught her, keeping her from tripping.

"How do you—" Cicero flushed, angry with herself for so noticeably reacting.

"Oh, come now," Wayland smiled his annoying smile. "We may play as though stuck in the past in Renaissance, but we can see what our neighbor's doing with the best of them. Magena Bedard wouldn't have called you in, speeding up

Banesska's arrival by nearly a season without good cause. And The Prince of Torts seemed to fit the bill."

"Excuse me," Magena, as if summoned to them by the mention of her name, abruptly stood before the pair. "Am I interrupting anything?"

"Not at all," Wayland said, patting Cicero's arm before releasing it. "Just keeping her company for you, Baroness. I see the balancers have begun seeing everyone's entourages out. Is the show about to start?"

While bodyguards were also signs of wealth signaling—a holdover from society pre-worldfall—none could be on hand for the actual ceremony, evidently making the proceedings that much more prestigious in their invitation-only status.

Cicero saw that Magena seemed to have not slept at all the night before.

"Are you okay?" she asked.

"Oh, I'm fine," Magena said. She locked eyes with Wayland, a look he seemed to think meant he should excuse himself.

"It's C.G.," Magena continued once they were as alone as they could be. "Cicero, he's been poisoned."

"He what!" Cicero started to pull away, but Magena caught her by both arms.

"He's fine," Magena said. "Luckily, a young technolomist was close by. The poor girl. She saw to C.G., and all that excitement, only to be with me visiting him at the clinic when I got word about the episode at the east borough dig site. She was friends with one of the diggers lost in the unfortunate accident."

"Oh, Magena, I'm sorry."

"Yes, thank you." Magena looked around. "Half the balancers on duty are still there, but we should be fine here with those left. Jerome Kantor on site is enough to keep things well in hand."

"Sure," Cicero took Magena's hand. "Is that all, Magena? Or is there something else on your mind?"

Magena looked deep into Cicero's eyes. She opened her mouth, held it open as she took a deep breath, then closed it.

"Oh, dear friend. I'm just so tired. I desperately miss my wife. Cassandra was made to be a baroness. I'm afraid I—"

The air in the hall filled with piercing screeches, seemingly from all over, as everyone covered their ears. Balancers, the police force of The Kingdom, rode hovering saddles, colloquially referred to as shriek bikes, while on duty.

"Magena?" Cicero asked, still covering her ears as the noise started moving away.

"What is—" Magena looked puzzled. Pale. She began walking toward the exit.

"It's Renaissance," a man in a gray wig said, walking up to them. A well-dressed young man came behind him. "There's some kind of attack happening."

All of the noise meant that the coronation of The Kingdom's newest baron no longer had any protection that wasn't privately paid for by people who had no vested interest in anyone's safety

beyond their own.

"No ceremony then, I guess?" Philip, the

well-dressed young man and star of the maligned

coronation, asked. "Straight to business it is."

A Digger's Woe

Outside of The Kingdom

2.4 km West of Lake Jacomo PW

(Pre-Worldfall)

(Four hours before the Coronation)

"Here's a plasma shovel and fob to your

mole, Earthmaster Batalon," the pale young boy

said as he handed Wade his equipment.

"Thanks, kid," Wade said, taking each in his

large brown hands. The plasma shovel was nothing

more than a long metal pole with a triangle-shaped

handle at one end until you turned it on, so Wade

slid it through the loop on the side of the pack on

his back. "But this isn't *my* mole. Just a loaner for today."

Wade's mole, an Echo-11 back in drydock getting a state-of-the-art stabilizer installed, was his pride and joy. As a digger, Wade had a lot of respect in The Kingdom. At seventeen, he was the youngest person ever to make it into the guild, and his father had spared no expense in setting him up with the best tools of the trade once Wade had gotten accepted.

A lot of math involved in being a digger— carving roads, walls, and various other structures out of solid rock without causing a cave-in involved intense precision. So, beyond being reasonably comfortable chairs suspended within a large, single wheel, the mole's sensors ran a lot of constant calculations needed to keep things structurally sound and safe, telling a digger where to cut or when to carve into the earth.

"Yes, sir," the boy smiled. "Your instructions are programmed into the *loaner* mole. It's to be Dig 17, I believe, sir."

"You got it," Wade said, giving the boy a nod as he walked on.

"Oh, and sir?" the boy called back. "Be careful on the road down to the site. Earthmaster Keylin says there have been a bunch of serpent sightings this week."

"Will do," Wade sighed. He didn't know which was worse, being on a site with Cray Keylin or the azure serpents. Azure serpents were the bane of the digger, sure. They wrecked entire cavern systems, burrowing massive tunnels through their rampages and, while there was no discernable sentience recorded in the creatures, would occasionally systematically destroy dig sites, eating through weeks' worth of carefully carved rock walls in hours. Azure serpents—their teal skin radiating beneath the earth gave them their name, though they resembled terrestrial crustaceans more than snakes —could grow to over twelve meters in length, so Wade had heard.

But Cray was, Cray.

Wade sat on the mole and hit the Start button on his fob, firing up his borrowed ride. He put the fob in the front pocket of his work coveralls and brought the mole's HUD into view. The schematics of the dig site popped up from the half-halo arc above the mole in a green hologram. Three flashing

blue lights indicated that Cray and the rest of

Wade's team had already headed the forty-eight

meters down.

Wade sighed again. It was going to be a long

shift.

*   *   *   *   *

"So I said, 'I told you it would fit just fine!'"

Cray barked a laugh as he finished his story. He

handed another wire from his mole to a small-

handed fellow next to him, who already held three

other wires, two tiny screws, and a small plastic

cover as he continued tooling beneath his work

vehicle.

"Ah, what a load of bull," a third worker spat. She worked another of the mole's plates loose across from Cray. "You've never spoken to Magena Bedard in your life."

"Now, don't ruin the story, Kinari," the small-handed man whined. "What'd she say next, Cray?" He shifted, excited, and dropped his assortment to the cavern floor.

"Dammit, Stev, look what ya did!" Cray shouted, standing from his work. Kinari stopped what she was doing and joined Stev in his hunt for the lost items.

"Idiot," she muttered. "If we don't return the mole in the exact same condition—"

Cray shushed the pair as Wade finished pulling to a stop on his mole.

"Guys," Wade nodded hello. "Kinari." The

trio shifted around in front of the disassembled

mole. "Problem with your ride?"

"It's all but handled, Batalon," Cray spoke

up. "Don't worry. We'll be down quick as you like."

"You got it," Wade said and took off again,

looking back to confirm his suspicions. Kinari and

Stev had returned to looking for whatever they'd

lost, but Cray locked eyes with Wade.

Shit, Wade thought and turned forward,

checking the mole's HUD for the rendezvous point.

He didn't want trouble with Cray again, but this felt

like familiar territory.

Because plasma shovels had difficulty

cutting through igneous rock, moles also came with

a small particle transmuter set to transform any

igneous rock into sedimentary. Rumor had it that Cray could reprogram the settings on a mole to change the problem stone into Cozer's Wine, an intense alcoholic beverage made illegal due to the hostility it brought out in folks. A month ago, Wade accidentally confirmed the rumor with supervisors when he caught Cray drunk on the job, landing Cray in trouble that he had seemingly managed to escape.

Things just got awkward, Wade thought. *Kinari's always been alright, but Stev is just a wet fart that follows Cray everywhere—does whatever Cray does. And* whatever *they're doing back there, Kinari's in on it, too.*

"Shit," Wade sighed, thinking aloud.

*   *   *   *   *

Kinari hurriedly slid her slender fingers over the cavern floor until she found the dropped screws. Landing on them, she quickly grabbed the plastic plate from Stev and began returning it to the mole.

"Hey, hold up," Cray said through gritted teeth as he snatched the plate back from her. "Just what do you think you're doing, partner?"

"We've still got plenty of our last batch, so what are we doing?" Kinari asked, staring Cray in the eyes as she did so. "I was already hesitant, but now, with that kid here? He got you busted once, and I'm not getting kicked out of the guild, Cray. I'm telling you, no. I'm out."

Stev, slowly sidling behind her while she argued with Cray, grabbed a stone from the cavern floor and bashed Kinari in the back of the head. Caught completely off-guard by the blow, Kinari fell limp to the ground, her black hair covering her face as blood from the wound pooled around her head.

"Fool!" Cray barked, clapping Stev on the side of the head. "She hadn't prepped her relay panel yet."

"Ah, she wasn't even going to," Stev grimaced, rubbing his head. "You heard her; she was worried about the kid ratting us out again."

"That punk," Cray snorted, removing the necessary components from the mole in double time. "And now I've got to do all the math here, so shut up a second." He began reprogramming the mole, rapidly typing and turning a dial one way,

then another.

Stev looked down the tunnel to ensure Wade

wasn't coming back up. A grin crossed his face that

matched the evil idea behind it. He bent down to

retrieve the bloodied rock and began to head down

the carved cavern hall.

"Where are you going?" Cray snapped.

"We'll be out in five."

"I was going to make sure about the kid,"

Stev moped, dropping his murder weapon.

"Don't worry about him," Cray said,

returning to work. "This is going to take care of

little problem Batalon. Besides, the Heirs are

moving in at our go."

Stev's smile returned.

*   *   *   *   *

Wade's feelings about the crew he'd found

himself on today faded to the back of his mind as he

focused on the job. Being a digger was important

throughout the Known Lands, particularly in The

Kingdom. Creating a new borough (used by the

population interchangeably with *burrow*, for

obvious reasons) meant safety in an unsafe world.

The walls of The Kingdom were sound, perfectly

suitable in keeping the monsters from the Waste and

the Unknown Land at bay—but there were other

dangers to be mindful of above ground. Air that

could become nearly unbreathable, seemingly on its

whim. Red lightning, enraged and murderous,

attacked from the sky out of nowhere. It happened less in The Kingdom than elsewhere in the Known Lands, but it did happen.

Boroughs were crafted precisely using strict guidelines—carved straight out of the earth if not a repurposed natural cavern, small underground villages some fifteen to twenty-three meters down —and could provide housing for up to five families. More if each family in question's headcount were small enough.

Seven boroughs were scattered throughout The Kingdom, with today's site becoming number eight.

Wade finished typing a complex series of formulas into his mole. Seconds later, PROXIMITY GRID ESTABLISHED ran across his HUD.

Wade read his go-ahead notification and

then checked the blinking lights for the rest of his

crew. The flashing lights indicated that they were

moving but not toward him. And only two of them

were still blinking.

Wade clicked the radio on his mole's dash

live.

"Sitrep."

Static was the only response.

"What's the holdup, Cray? Is everyone

alright? Guys?"

The tunnel Wade was in rocked heavily, as

though the world were set up on a giant blanket, and

someone had come along and given it a rolling flip.

Microseconds later, his senses filled with endless

roaring and falling dust, rock, and flame.

Wade's dig site had seemingly come to life and swallowed him in an end of days rage.

* * * * *

"Get with it, fool!" Cray hurried the much smaller Stev through one of the unaffected tunnels with a push. "How much time do you think we've got before Kantor and his balancers are down here mapping out the scene?"

Stev stumbled, caught himself with his palms, and ran on all fours before uprighting. "I'm hurrying!"

The pair came to a T-shape in the tunnel and headed right. As Cray and Stev furthered their way, the tunnel became less polished. Lanterns still needed to be installed, so new was this carved

cavern, and light became scarce.

"I don't like this, Cray," Stev said under his

breath.

"Shut it," Cray said, holding his bio torch

toward the darkness, catching the reflected eyes of

dozens of faces. "They're here."

*   *   *   *   *

Wade woke up. His left leg, or the pain from

it, is what awakened him. He had no idea how long

he'd been unconscious.

It was completely black in the pocket of

stone he was in—save for the angrily flashing

dashboard of his mole—but there was still

breathable air, so he decided he couldn't have been out for too long.

That wasn't a tunnel collapse, he thought. *That was an explosion.*

Wade assessed many things all at once. He'd seen Cray, Stev, and Kinari up to something. Maybe they'd miscalculated when converting their moles into Cozer wine distilleries, but that seemed unlikely. The amount of damage and the size of the explosion didn't fit that scenario.

Which made Wade think this was intentional.

He groaned loudly, wincing as he felt the damage to his leg. While the rubble surrounding Wade hadn't managed to crush him—by some miracle—it had seemingly shattered his left shin.

My body is quickly going to go into shock, Wade thought. *I don't need Kendra here to tell me that much. Though, her Technolomist kit would be awfully convenient right about now.*

Wade screamed as he attempted to turn his body toward the mole. The pain from his leg, his shinbone like loose gravel, nearly caused him to pass out again. Then, with tears streaming down his face, the young boy took deep breaths and blew them out slowly, attempting to push the pain to the side. He couldn't will it away, it was far too intense, but maybe he could set it in the back of his mind like he would a cumbersome formula. Still aware of the pain but not letting it consume his focus.

I've got to reach the mole and call for help.

He shifted his whole body again, eliciting

another primal scream that, at first, he didn't

recognize as coming from his own throat. Wade fell

to his side, holding his leg gently as he looked at the

mole.

Huh, he thought. *Either the mole's power*

supply is about to give out, meaning my lights are

going, or I'm losing consciousness again.

As it turned out, it was both.

* * * * *

The Heirs of the Earth continued piling

through the collapsed wall that Cray had provided,

numbering nearly forty strong by Stev's count,

though he had lost track a little bit once he ran out

of tallying fingers and toes. (Stev acted as Cray's porter. An essential job in the Digger's Guild, to be sure, but much less reliant on mathematics.)

"Where they all headed?" he asked Cray as the men kept filing past.

"Don't worry about it, wart," a 6'6" giant barked as he stepped out from the dark passage.

"Don't mind him, Portman," Cray spoke to the man behind a big grin while staring daggers at Stev. "Everything is ready. If you can get in place, it's all timed to go down during the coronation."

"It's all going according to plan," Portman said, bumping Stev as he walked by. "The azure serpent got us to your wall—her carcass is about ten meters back when you lead your people to it later. Keplinger arrived three days ago on Banesska's crew. He'll have handled the rest. You just return to your places, and everything will stay smooth."

Stev rubbed his shoulder where Portman had bumped into him, falling behind the larger men as they walked back toward the entrance to the site. He still didn't understand why Heirs only went by their last names—Cray had explained that it was a pride thing. Ties to the world before the fall, or some such. The entire thing seemed silly to Stev, but he followed Cray's lead. Always. Understanding their partners, or even the plan beyond his part in it, had never been a prerequisite.

* * * * *

Wade came to slowly, as though shifting from one dream into another in the comfort of his own home. His bedroom, it seemed, was filled with rocks and a dull blue light emanating from somewhere, though, and there was a strange squelching sound, as though someone was watching him sleep while eating an overripe melon.

His mind snapped back to reality, and he sat upright with a jolt. He was still in the collapsed dig site, and the light was coming from a long, thin azure serpent, a milky fluid coming from its grasshopper-like mouth as it seemed to feed on his wounded leg: *fnnnk, fnnnk.*

"Get off!" Wade yelled, kicking at the creature with his good leg. The azure serpent screeched and skittered away toward the wreckage of Wade's mole. As it did, Wade had a sudden flash, a vision of the creature discovering him unconscious, bleeding out, and near death. Though it went against its base instinct to stay away from him, it opted to aid Wade before the beating of his heart stopped entirely.

That's when Wade noticed his leg, shattered in the explosion, no longer hurt.

The creature had saved Wade's life.

He stood and walked over to where the baby azure serpent was squeaking inside the mole. In terror, it had confusedly climbed into the wreckage rather than escape into the stone.

"Hey, look," Wade whispered, gently shushing the creature's cries. "I'm sorry. You just freaked me out, is all. I'm accustomed to your giant-sized cousins eating up my dig sites. Not little guys like you saving me."

Wade sat cross-legged in front of the mole.

He grabbed his radio in a futile attempt to reach out

for help but to no avail. Finally, he stooped down to

look toward the blue light from under the mole's

seat. The crying had subsided, replaced with what

sounded like a purring clack: *fnnnk, fnnnk*.

"Can you come back out here, please?"

Wade asked, putting his hand out toward the

serpent. "I promise I won't hurt you again."

The creature skittered out, slowly at first, its

hundreds of tiny legs tik-tik-tiking across the metal

of the mole until it reached Wade's outstretched

hand. It leaned up the front three sections of its

armored body to get closer, seemingly to weigh the

danger of the situation, then touched its head to

Wade's hand.

Wade then got another vision, a group of

men torturing a giant azure serpent, forcing it to dig

beneath The Kingdom's gates until an explosion

killed it. The men then climbed through a hole

caused by the blast and left.

Wade shook his head free of the vision,

sitting hard on the cave floor. Then, after he could

think clearly again, he began to plan.

"Listen, little man. Little Fennick," Wade

wasn't entirely sure why he named the creature.

Maybe, just then, he needed a friend. "Fennick.

Huh. S'good a name as any, I guess. We've got to

get out of here, and I will need your help to make

that happen."

The Myth of Coin: Dark Deeds

The Barony of Renaissance

Bonner Springs, Kansas PW

(Pre-Worldfall)

(Ten minutes before the Coronation)

Clutch Halpscome walked the wooden

fence's catwalk, pacing to fend off sleep. He ran his

tired hands over a face that looked old when he was

half his current age, trying to wake himself up.

Clutch was the nighttime ward of the Southern

entrance into Renaissance. He preferred the night

shift because you didn't have to contend with the

gates being open at night, which meant next to no

people to deal with either.

Clutch liked that.

Having worked his shift, Clutch was doing a double, covering the Eastern gate for his poker buddy, Smithland Vogue. Or Smitty, as Clutch referred to him, because, while it was customary to remake oneself in Renaissance—including a new identity to fit the Ren faire theme—Clutch couldn't bring himself to call a grown man Smithland Vogue.

Doing so would remind him too much of all the capes, the era of superheroes and villains of the 90s that went out of fashion once the world fell. Clutch believed they had silly names to go with their sillier costumes, and a name like Smithland Vogue was more of that time. Whereas Smitty was a guy you could play cards with in this one.

Maybe thinking about his younger years—

the superpowered folks with their powers—made

Clutch not immediately clock the three trailer mag-

lifts heading toward his post.

He'd wonder on that later in the day, amidst

all the misery and bloodshed, and then for the rest

of his life after.

The trailers were old, pre-worldfall

eighteen-wheeler loads, converted with mag-lifts in

place of tires that let the entire thing defy gravity in

a way that Clutch never understood. The mag-lifts

were how Banesska's Traveling Game managed the

traveling part. Still, with another day of carnival fun

left to go, those mag-lifts were currently coming at

Clutch's gate and coming in fast.

"East door going hot," Clutch yelled into a radio hooked on the shoulder of his jacket. "Repeat, East door going hot! Double-time!"

He ran for the ladder and climbed to the ground, heading for the hatch tucked under the catwalk that housed the gate's controls.

"This a drill, Clutch?" came a voice over the radio. "Because I'm already dealing with Miss de Winter running off with the Baron's horse, and—"

"No, dammit!" Clutch barked back. He hit a black button followed by another yellow one. "Three trailers, nearly on us. Hot, hot, hot!"

As the gates closed with the push of the black button, the yellow button fired up a pulse field that formed about a meter in front of the ten-meter wooden fence that kept trouble out of Renaissance.

It would not do so today.

*　*　*　*　*

The Barony of Tuggett's Knee

The Temple

"I don't think canceling your coronation will
be necessary," Cicero said as the hall began to fill
with murmuring guests. "Will it, Magena?"

"Oh, um, I think we can still—" Magena
looked past Cicero toward the entrance to The
Temple. "We'll proceed as planned, Philip. Please,
excuse me a moment."

As Magena wandered off, Philip asked
Cicero, "I know that the eastern edge of Tuggett's

Knee runs along Scar City's border, but I assume

we're still safe here. Are we? Safe with the

balancers gone?"

"There's no need for concern," Cicero

absently answered as she watched Magena talk to

other worried nobles on her way.

"Okay, then," Philip clapped his hands.

"Renault, the show goes on, it seems. Where should

I be right now?"

The gray-wigged man led his master away

as Cicero slowly turned about the room, taking in

the sights, sounds, and smells with new interest.

There was a palpable tension. Cicero knew

there was an emergency, to be sure, but that was

elsewhere. Yet something felt off in The Temple to

Cicero, too.

The upper crust of The Kingdom began to get anxious, with more than a few heading for the exit to get within reach of their bodyguards.

Well, the show may go on, but it will likely play to an empty house. Cicero thought.

Someone started shouting then. Cicero couldn't quite make out what was being said and had no hope of doing so once the crowd began screaming.

*   *   *   *   *

The Barony of Tuggett's Knee

Technolomist Clinic #3

Crossroads District PW

(Pre-Worldfall)

Kendra paced the front lobby of the clinic, just outside of C.G. Banesska's room. She was trying to keep her mind off of Wade while she waited for Sepia to meet her there.

A man with a long silver beard wearing a floor-length purple coat, the Technolomists' garb, brushed past her as he headed toward the patient's room.

"I'm sorry for your loss, Miss Lawden," he said, stopping before the door.

"Thank you, sir," Kendra said, her eyes growing wet again with tears. She continued to pace.

"Finally," C.G. called from his bed. "Doctor Odinson, I'm feeling fine now. When might I be able to leave?"

"Well, now, let's be cautious," Dr. Odinson said, entering the room. "I believe Miss Lawden's theory is sound, that this may not have been an attempt on your life, but I've still a few screens I'd like to do."

"Fine, fine." C.G. sighed. "I'm just getting antsy. By the way, do you know what's become of the Battle Board rig I was brought in with?"

"The onsite technolomists gathered it once they got you into bed," Dr. Odinson said. "I'm sure that—"

Kendra stopped listening and went inward as she walked, trying desperately to push down the rock that weighed heavily on her heart.

Wade, she thought. *Gone. We have always been three—he, Sepia, and I. The Three Musketeers. The Knights Astray.*

Going back to childhood, the three of them would always find ways to sneak away, typically after dark. Their nights astray. Sepia, leaning into her Renaissance upbringing, first christened them with the tweak of *nights* to *Knights*. This was before Sepia lost her mother, making Sepia's father and her uncle, the Baron of Renaissance, much warier. They hadn't been the Knights Astray for a long time after that.

Not until last night.

Kendra began to cry again, the heaviness in

her chest more than she could bear.

* * * * *

The Barony of Renaissance

Sepia knew better than to leave by the

eastern gate because Clutch was working. Clutch,

her father's best friend, was basically part

bloodhound. There's no chance she would have

gotten out of Renaissance through East Gate.

But South Gate was another story.

Sepia's father, Horatio de Winter, was a

large man—less tall so much than wide around the

middle—so his horse, Hippolyta, was a magnificent

animal. Still, with everyone in the barony distracted by Banesska's Traveling Game, it had taken Sepia longer to saddle and get Hippolyta to mind her lead than it had to sneak out of the barony on her father's horse.

They'd gone roughly a quarter of a kilometer, hugging the treeline as best as Sepia could manage while remaining out of Clutch's sight, hoping to return to the road east.

Chk-chk, Sepia attempted to nudge Hippolyta into continuing once the large mare stopped still. "Come on, girl," Sepia choked back a sob, knowing what emotions she'd have to fully confront at the technolomist clinic. "Kendra's waiting. Let's go."

But Hippolyta wouldn't be moved forward.

In fact, the horse trodded *backward* a few steps.

Sepia looked to see what had Hippolyta's attention just as one of Banesska's mag-lifted trailers slammed into East Gate. The ensuing explosion as the speeding trailer blasted through the pulse field caused Hippolyta to rear back, nearly throwing Sepia to the ground.

Hippolyta tore off in a southeastern direction, ripping through the forest as she escaped such wanton destruction.

Sepia, letting Hippolyta have her lead, hugged tightly to the steed as flames from the wreckage engulfed South Gate some sixty meters away.

And two more trailers slowed to a stop

before the carnage.

*   *   *   *   *

The Barony of Tuggett's Knee

The Temple

The plan was sound. Wait for the signal,

then bust into the hall, weapons ready. The way had

been made clear of any danger of being caught, and

the small room, a storage space in the world before,

had served quite well as a hiding space in this one.

But the signal didn't come.

The men grew impatient.

With coin heavy in their pockets, eager to be

spent, the local thugs and gathered brigands grew

bloodthirsty.

When it became too much—the hobnobbing

and the gossiping coming from The Kingdom's elite

society on the other side of the door, Tip Coleman

led a veritable who's who of Scar City denizens out

to say hello.

"Blood for The Prince of Torts!" Tip cried

out as he and a dozen men barreled through the

crowd of startled onlookers, hacking and stabbing

as they went.

The cry rose from the killers and thieves:

"BLOOD FOR THE PRINCE!"

Tip sneered at the middle-aged couple,

tripping over their own brightly colored robes and

gowns to get away from his motley crew, then

laughed, "The Prince of Torts sends his regards!"

However, the laughter died still in his throat

at the sight of the bard.

Tip scanned the Temple, fearing he'd see his

end in a barrage of balancers, but calmed himself

when he didn't.

His laugh returned.

"Come on, boys," he smirked. "I don't know

about you, but I wanna see what it's like to gut a

bard."

*   *   *   *   *

Outside of The Kingdom

Wreckage of the East Borough Dig Site

A half-dozen moles and twice as many

diggers worked to clear the site's entrance of heavy

stone. The air was filled with only the sounds of

digger tools, plasma shovels, and quarry bins—

large trucks with long high-edged beds that would

shimmy the rocks while getting precise readings,

searching for any useful mineral deposits. The

diggers were somber in their work, having

potentially lost two of their own to the wreckage.

Still, their guild lived by the motto "no stone

unturned" nonetheless.

Their work was slowed by the immense

carcass of the azure serpent that had been blown to

pieces.

Shinji Orito, a balancer known for his even-

headedness and keen mind, oversaw the scene as

the diggers worked, managing the resources and the technolomists on standby should any survivors be discovered and rescued.

The Balancer and Digger Guilds often found themselves in lockstep cooperation whenever a tragedy occurred, if not as often other times.

Chief Kantor had posted Shinji and two other balancers, Vessig and Marcus, before heading back to The Temple with every other balancer on shift to oversee The Coronation.

"So that I'm clear, Earthmaster Keylin," Shinji said, his eyes remaining on the azure serpent's corpse instead of the man sitting behind him. "The creature burrowed into the dig site, straight into a thus far unidentified methane patch, causing the explosion that brought down the entire

cavern?"

"Unmapped boom patches happen more

than ya think!" Stev barked. He continued shifting

as the technolomist, a young woman of

twentysomething, tried to scan him for injuries until

Cray shot him a look.

"I'm sure they do," Shinji said, finally

facing the pair. He caught the look between Cray

and Stev. Something felt off. "Unless you've found

anything, Doctor, I believe we've finished with your

services. Thank you." Shinji, the edge of his red

cloak in hand, extended his armored arm to point

the technolomist away.

The young woman bowed, finished her readings, then bunched her purple robe above her feet to leave, rejoining her crew.

"It's just as we said," Cray began, smiling what he must have thought was a reassuring smile at Shinji, "And the onsite recorder can confirm—"

"Oh, we've talked to the boy," Shinji interrupted. "He said that some twenty minutes after Earthmaster Batalon arrived, an explosion occurred in or around Dig 17 and that moments after, you two—"

"*Balancer Orito,*" Balancer Vessig's voice rang from the radio built into Shinji's armored cuirass.

"Go ahead," Shiinji responded with a touch to his chest.

"Better get down here," Balancer Vessig

said. *"The diggers found another asure serpent*

tunnel."

"A second one?" Shinji asked, bewildered.

"Yes, sir. Only they say this one was dug

after the cavern collapsed. And it's much smaller."

"Keep these two here," Shinji told Balancer

Marcus as he strode quickly past him, pointing at

the Cray and Stev.

Something *was* off, indeed.

* * * * *

The Barony of Tuggett's Knee

Technolomist Clinic #3

Where are you, Sepia? Kendra wondered.

She waited for Sepia outside; well, in truth, she was asked to wait for her outside, as Kendra's pacing was aggravating to numerous clinic staff members.

It was always night after the world fell, and the streetlights in The Kingdom stayed ever-lit, fighting to stave off that darkness. Certain baronies could afford to keep homes lit as well, dressing their day-to-day with a semblance of night and day. Still, while she kept the clinics in suitable lighting, Kendra always admired Magena Bedard for not wasting energy when she didn't need to.

Wasting energy as I am doing now, Kendra thought. She promptly sat beneath a streetlight and began calming her breathing. At Kendra's third slow intake of breath, Sepia came barreling out of the darkness and onto the street, riding Hippolyta at a breakneck pace.

"Anyone?" Sepia shouted from atop her goliath steed. "Everyone! Call the balancers, all of them! Renaissance is under attack!"

"Sepia, you're bleeding!" Kendra yelled, running toward her friend.

Sepia drew Hippolyta to a slow trot and then hopped down. Her face had long streaks of blood from the branches of the forest scraping her face in her hurried pace through them.

"Kendra," Sepia said, hugging her. "Oh, Kendra, there's no time. I can't believe it about Wade. What we've lost. I'm sorry, truly, but I must raise the guard!"

"The balancers should be at The Temple,"

Kendra explained, wiping the blood from her

friend's cheeks with the sleeve of her robe, "but the

shriek bikes took out moments ago."

"I came from the south," Sepia said,

climbing back on her father's horse. "Maybe they

already know. Still, I must make sure. Are you

coming?"

Kedra followed her up onto Hippolyta

without saying another word.

*   *   *   *   *

The Barony of Tuggett's Knee

The Temple

Cicero whipped her long red sash around,

the hidden weights within causing severe damage to

her intended targets, hitting one thug in the throat

before spinning to catch his comrade in the face,

shattering his nose in a fury of spattered blood.

"Defend yourselves or get out!" Cicero

barked orders to the panicked crowd before

cartwheeling her way into a spin kick at another of

the brutish attackers.

Where is Magena? Cicero wondered,

worriedly scanning the room as she dodged the

homemade blades of two more—a large red-haired

fighter and a balding dwarf—from the band of

rogues that had set upon them.

Cicero brought her focus back on the task at

hand, wrapping the large red-haired fighter's hand

tight around his wrist, then bringing her knee up into it as she yanked down. The man's bones splintered, and he dropped his weapon. Cicero freed her sash and pirouetted away with another spin and a flourish, narrowly dodging the dwarf's attack and losing him amidst the escaping crowd.

"Cicero, look out!" came a scream.

Cicero spun at the warning, causing a man wielding a machete to miss his mark but still catch her with a gouge across her deltoid. She swung her sash with her good arm, circling it almost like a lasso as the man's eyes went wide and then narrowed.

"Gonna gut you, bard," Tip sneered. "That gash in your arm's gonna feel like a gentle breeze time I'm through."

Though Cicero continued swinging her weighted sash, her eyes darted to the entrance to see who had called out. She saw Wayland de Winter's niece and another girl ride into The Temple on the most giant horse Cicero had ever seen.

The great hall had emptied of all non-combatants, leaving only Cicero and three opponents standing, the man with the machete and another two she noticed coming from her sides trying to flank her. Cicero began to pivot sideways as she swung her sash.

*   *   *   *   *

"You better hop down, Kendra," Sepia whispered.

As Kendra slid off Hippolyta, Sepia spurred the great horse toward the battle.

"Kii-yah!" Hippolyta ran forward, filling The Temple with the sound of her shod hooves as she quickly covered the space between the entrance and the fight.

Then, to Sepia's eyes, everything moved in slow motion.

The man in front of Cicero turned, startled, toward Sepia as she bore down Hippolyta on top of and over a second man, the one to Cicero's right. Sepia watched Cicero feint forward, then flip her sash into the throat of the third man attempting to surround her. Cicero quickly went from being outnumbered to standing against one final foe.

"I-I surrender," Tip screamed, throwing down his machete. "I give up!"

He dropped to his knees and put his hands behind his head.

Cicero wrapped her sash around her waist and approached her prisoner as Sepia looked back at the mangled body of the man she'd run down. His head was twisted at the neck at an odd angle, and he wasn't moving.

"Sepia. Sepia!" Kendra repeated until her friend snapped to attention.

"I'm okay," Sepia said, though her eyes were welling with tears. She looked around then and saw the bodies strewn throughout The Temple. Dozens of people, their colorful robes and shaws covered in blood, as though there had been a grand

sleepover. If not for all the gore.

"Girls, I'm going to need your help," Cicero

said. She knelt on the back of the now unarmed and

prostrated Tip, binding his hands with one long

cylindrical cuff. "I need to check if there are any

survivors in here."

"I'm a technolomist," Kendra said. "Well,

almost. Studying to be. I can help."

"Okay, get started," Cicero said. "Sepia, if

this guy moves, have your horse step on him." Tip

whined, face down. "I've got to find Baroness

Bedard as well."

"Hello! I need balancers, quickly!" a boy

was shouting from outside.

"Is that—" Sepia's voice quivered.

"Wade?!" Kendra screamed.

Cicero watched a young man carrying a plasma shovel handle enter The Temple. Sepia slid off of her horse and chased after Kendra as the two of them almost tackled him to the ground in hugs.

Cicero got her prisoner up and marched him toward the trio.

"I'm okay, I'm okay!" he said.

Magena walked in behind the friends and Cicero, seeing her, visibly relaxed somewhat.

"Baroness," Cicero said.

Magena continued walking, surveying the horrific scene with dark, sad eyes. She wore a few fresh bruises, and her clothes were torn. She locked on Philip's ravaged body, hardly making it out as his. It was buried under the body of his manservant, who seemingly died trying to protect him.

"It seems our new baron's accession has ended prematurely," she whispered, choking back a sob.

"Baroness?" Cicero repeated, touching Magena's shoulder.

"Cicero, I'm so happy you're okay," Magena said, her face still in a dreamlike shock but with a flash of awareness. "Children, you as well. But there is no time. Get to safety. Cicero, we'll leave this man in custody at the Technolomist Clinic for now."

"Magena," Cicero said. "Where are the balancers? What else has happened?"

"It's happening still, so we must hurry,"

Magena choked. "Renaissance is burning."

*   *   *   *   *

The Barony of Renaissance

After the first trailer crashed through,

Portman and his fellow Heirs of the Earth made

short work of what remained of Renaissance's main

gate. They were thirty-six strong, pouring out of the

remaining two mag-lifted trailers and armed with

staves, blades, and crossbows.

"Keplinger, grab the beacon," Portman

shouted to a broad-chested man dressed in blue and

green coveralls. "You're with me. Everyone else,

you have your orders. Eyes track!"

"Arms attack!" Thirty-five men yelled in

unison as they ran through the flaming wreckage

and into Renaissance.

*　　*　　*　　*　　*

"Get balancers out to Renaissance, now!"

Clutch shouted into the shortwave radio, throwing

the communicator once the message was through.

He'd lost five good people getting to the guard

hutch and was taking it out on the equipment.

Clutch pulled Wes Harvester, who was

looking worse for wear as a lump over his right eye

continued growing, up off the floor by his arm.

"Time to go, Wes," Clutch said.

Wes only groaned in response, but his feet carried him on.

Clutch managed a six-foot spear into a battle position once Wes could walk unaided again. His head stayed at a steady pivot as the pair carefully made their way back outside.

Fires raged as the heraldry of Renaissance— colorful flags, tents, and banners by the score—fed the flames easily and readily.

A trio of thugs rushed them from beyond the smoke, and Clutch only just got his spear around in time to skewer the one on his left, but the weapon stuck deep and pulled from his hands as Clutch's victim fell dead. A bo staff caught him in the ear, and his vision went white.

Wes dove into the assailant with the staff,

his short, thin blade going to work on the man's

torso, making squishing noises in concert with

Clutch passing out.

* * * * *

Portman and Keplinger snuck through the

carnage their brother Heirs were causing, sticking to

what few shadows remained in the burning barony.

Keplinger toted a medium-sized black box

following Portman's lead as the two hustled.

Portman held them back at the corner of a

building as two people completely engulfed in

flames ran past them. Once the way was clear again,

Portman pointed toward a building across the street.

"That should do," he said.

Then he pulled something that no one in Renaissance had seen in decades from his inside coat pocket.

A gun.

*　*　*　*　*

Cicero led their motley crew from the back of a quarter horse named Smoke, who she'd borrowed from a technolomist from the clinic. Smoke wasn't nearly the size of Hippolyta. Still, he managed both Cicero and Magena—who had both of her arms wrapped around Cicero's waist— sharing the ride. The larger horse carried the two younger girls while the presumed dead digger, Wade, brought up the year in his mole.

None of the kids would stay behind, no matter what Magena ordered.

The baroness remained quiet as they sped toward Renaissance, only speaking through the radio for updates on the rare chance she could get anyone.

The attackers weren't known to any balancers so far as was being reported. They came in fast, numbered around forty, armed, and with seemingly random destructive intent.

"We've taken out most of the assailants," Balancer Kantor said over the radio. His voice was like gravel falling over gravel. *"But the leader and at least one other are holed up in the old hospital."*

"What on earth for?" Magena asked. "It's a derelict stripped of anything useful decades ago."

"*I can't say, ma'am,*" Balancer Kantor quickly replied. "*But I'm heading in to find out.*"

Magena put the radio inside her robe. "Hurry, Cicero."

* * * * *

Sepia couldn't catch her breath once they arrived in Renaissance. Her home had been ripped away, and a war zone of burning wreckage and mangled earth had taken its place. The young woman she had been was gone, leaving her body lingering like a ghost around her friends.

"Wade, take her," Kendra said, coaxing Sepia toward him. "I've got to see if I can help."

Wade nodded. "I'm sure your father is okay," he said to Sepia as he hugged her. "Your uncle, too."

This snapped Sepia out of her daze. "My father!" She pushed off of Wade, shouting. "Dad? Daddy!"

"Muzzle her!" came a harsh whisper from the line of people watching the scene at the old hospital.

Then a loud bang rang out from somewhere inside. The crowd fell apart as people dove for cover. Cicero pulled Magena down and leaned over her, looking toward the building. "Get down!" she yelled.

Wade pulled Sepia around the corner of his

mole, sitting them behind its seat. Kendra doubled

back and over to them, diving to the ground and

bumping the mole.

"How in the world do they have guns?" she

asked. "I don't even know if—"

A chittering came from somewhere within

the seat of the mole, causing Kendra to jump back.

"I'll explain everything," Wade said, pulling

Kendra's hand back as she went to look inside the

seat. "Please, just later. One crisis at a time!"

*   *   *   *   *

Portman peeked around the corner of the

door. He wasn't sure if he'd hit the big man, but he

thought so. Maybe not a killing shot, it was too dark, but the man seemed to drop like he'd been shot.

"How much longer?" he asked over his shoulder.

"Two minutes," Keplinger said. He had opened the black box, unfolded it into a cross on the floor of the old building, and was now painting sigils into each section with his own blood. "Are you sure this is high enough?"

"It will have to be," Portman said from the door. "I'll buy you your two minutes. Eyes track!"

Keplinger shouted their customary response to an otherwise empty room.

*　*　*　*　*

The truth of the matter was Clutch

Halpscome saved Jerome Kantor's life. Clutch had

woken up dazed to find Wes Harvester dead.

Luckily for Clutch, Wes had taken the other two of

their surviving attackers with him before he fell.

Clutch didn't have time to mourn his friend, though,

as he noticed Balancer Kantor heading into the old

hospital alone.

Clutch got up, shook off some lingering

dizziness, gathered his spear, and joined the

balancer.

"Good lord, citizen," Jerome said as he

lowered his ion bat. "Get back with the others."

"Can't do that, I'm afraid," Clutch said, still

in step with the balancer. "This lot came for me and

mine. There's hell to pay, and I aim to be the debt collector."

Jerome just grunted, understanding. The pair warily made their way into the dark building. Echoes abounded in the hospital, making their quarry reasonably easy to track.

As Jerome and Clutch exited the stairwell on the fourth floor, Clutch heard a sound he hadn't heard in this new world. It was a noise from his previous life as a soldier before the world fell.

The cocking of a pistol.

Reacting without thought, Clutch pulled Jerome to the floor as the gun fired. To his credit, Jerome stayed unmoving and silent as their attacker moved in to confirm the kill, shouting something about eyes to someone in the room behind him.

Three steps closer was all Jerome was going to allow the killer. He thumbed his ion bat to life and threw it toward the invader's dark shape.

BAM! Came another shot, followed by a third. Clutch didn't wait to see if either man hit his target. He only knew *he* hadn't been hit, so Clutch followed the balancer's lead, pushing up from their position and diving at their prey.

* * * * *

The shooting had stopped, but Balancer Kantor hadn't radioed an all-clear, so the crowd outside stayed tucked out of sight of the old hospital.

"Baroness, stay down," Cicero instructed, then cautiously rose to her feet. She called over to three people who shared Kantor's armored garb. "Balancers, I plan to enter after your commander. I'd take it as a kindness if you'd follow me."

The four of them double-timed into the building as stealthily as their speed would allow, following the sounds of a battle upstairs.

Weighing their need for surprise against their need to see in the dark hallways of the abandoned building, Cicero asked if any of her party had a bio torch. The balancer bringing up their rear moved up, bio torch in hand.

"Sorry, ma'am," the woman said, passing it to Cicero. "It's half-drained."

Cicero stopped her group and waited a thirty count there in the dark. There was still only the sound of fighting from somewhere above them, but that was all. She flicked the bio torch on.

"Let's go," she said, lighting their path as they resumed their pace.

Everything became clear as they came up the stairs to the fourth floor. Balancer Kantor and another man were in the throes of a vicious fight with a giant of a man who had a broken spear through his left thigh. The balancer's right arm hung useless as he attempted the pin the larger man against the wall by his throat with his left arm. The third man was riddling the giant with punch after punch to his ribs. Blood was everywhere.

Cicero hardly had time to take in the scene

before Balancer Kantor shouted, "We've got this!

Go stop whatever's happening in the room!"

A loud hum began then as green and purple

lights shone from beyond the nearby doorway.

Cicero nodded and pointed to the balancer

closest to her. "You, help here. You two, with me."

As they cleared the corner of the door,

Cicero first saw into the room. The swirling lights

were hard to look at. Not because they were bright

but because there was a tangibility to them, like

colored mucus.

Cicero was able to dodge a stream of

whatever it was, but the balancer behind her was not

as lucky. The purple-green light touched his right

shin, causing him to scream and drop to the floor.

Amid all the spinning lights, Cicero saw a man sitting with his legs crossed and either hand open, palms up on his knees.

He was smiling at her.

"Stop . . . whatever you're doing, and put your hands—" Cicero started to yell as the hum grew louder, and then louder still, until ending in an ear-splitting crescendo.

Within seconds, the smiling figure's skin turned burnt black and then scattered in millions of torn flakes as though blown by a wind that wasn't present.

Then all was quiet.

*   *   *   *   *

Portman let go of the freshly dead woman's throat, and her lifeless body hit the floor. He then limped over to Jerome and put his massive hands over the downed balancer's face, a thumb over each eye. Jerome screamed, and blood continued drooling from his mouth.

Portman paused before finishing off the Chief Balancer as the hum from the other room had stopped.

"Heh, it's done," Portman's smile split his face. "You can't escape what's coming now. Gauntlet knows where you are, and he'll be on his way with the soul mark to guide him. And all this, what I done? It will seem like a kiddie's birthday party."

Portman made to finish the job of Jerome

then, but Clutch surprised him. He'd gotten to his

feet, holding the other end of the broken spear, and

shoved nearly two feet of the pointed handle

through the giant's neck. Then, the nighttime ward

of the Southern entrance into Renaissance fell back

to the floor.

"Debt's clear," Clutch muttered.

* * * * *

Fires were contained and put out, and people

began searching for any family and friends

unaccounted for. Balancers came in borrowed units

from all over The Kingdom to help secure things,

and technolomists scoured the scene as the citizens

of Renaissance came out to gather their wounded and dead.

Cicero helped bring the wounded out of the old hospital. She was carrying one end of the stretcher that held the balancer who had been downed by the bizarre lights. Cicero was no technolomist, but even she knew by looking that the man's leg looked dead from the knee down. It was pure white, and the veins inside had run black. The man to whom the leg belonged seemed unconscious but was muttering gibberish in his sleep.

Kendra took Cicero's place manning the stretcher with a weary nod, and they were off.

Cicero saw Baroness Bedard a few yards away from everyone speaking into a radio and made her way over.

"Maggy," Cicero began, seeing that Magena was finished.

"That was Baron Dibbek, which means now all key members of The Quorum are up to speed," Magena said, placing her radio back in her robes. "Gods, I need a drink."

"Make that two. One for each of us." Cicero nodded. "So, what do you make of this? Do you think it's the work of your Prince of Torts?"

Magena began walking back toward the crowd of people.

"From what Jerome says, and the sentry Master Halpscome concurs, this is some unknown enemy. Someone called Gauntlet."

Cicero inhaled deeply through her nose, letting the breath out slowly.

"A new threat then," Cicero said. "I'm only one person, Maggy. I can't investigate both The Prince and whoever this Gauntlet is. I'll need some help. Particularly—"

"Yes, yes, Cicero," Magena interrupted. Then she, too, took a deep breath. "I'm sorry. I know from overtaxed. Let me help Renaissance today. Let's not worry about The Prince."

"Not worry?" Cicero asked, shocked. "The entire reason I'm here—"

"And now something bigger has happened!" Magena shouted. "Cicero, Renaissance is burning! The Kingdom is under attack on a level beyond *any* kind of front it's ever faced since The Shift. Criminals fighting for scraps in the shadows are just . . . they are not a priority any longer."

Baroness Bedard walked away.

"I'll go check on our prisoner," Cicero called after her. "See if I can't find a connection. Baroness."

Magena turned back around, and the two women locked eyes. Magena nodded curtly and then continued on her way.

Epilogue

The Barony of Tugget's Knee

3:00 AM

The Inn At World's Fair

(Tavern)

It was always dark in the world after the fall, so having a clandestine meeting during the wee hours didn't provide any more cover of darkness, but it did mean fewer eyes.

Wade's family owned The Inn At World's Fair, so he was happy to have everyone gather someplace where he could control things, even partially. He grew tired of pacing in the inn's kitchen, so he went outside to meet his friends.

Minutes later, he saw a young woman coming down a side street rather than the main thoroughfare.

"Kendra," he said, hugging her as she got close. "The others aren't here yet."

"I'm a touch early," Kendra said. "I wanted to check in on our patient."

"Shh," Wade looked around. "Sepia knows about him, but her new instructor doesn't."

"So talk fast before they get here," Kendra said, but also looked over her shoulder. "How is he sleeping?"

"Fennick is doing great, thanks. He's sleeping much better in that incubator we rigged."

Kendra smiled but didn't speak as the rest of their party had arrived.

*   *   *   *   *

"Sepia trusts you," Cicero began, hardly

believing she was speaking to three children in the

middle of the night, around a table in a bar. Without

their parents' knowledge, let alone consent. "And

along with the bit of time we've spent together, that

makes me feel like I can trust you, too.

"I asked you all to meet me here in secret

because, outside of the people in this room, I'm not

sure who else in The Kingdom I can trust right

now."

Sepia had her black hair pulled back into a

single braid. It came just around her neck onto her

shoulder, in line with her teacher's, if much shorter.

"My father says it, too," Sepia said. "Since the onslaught in Renaissance, distrust is everywhere."

Wade and Kendra both nodded.

"Okay, so what's this about?" Kendra asked.

"I'd like to compare notes. Baroness Bedard called me early to The Kingdom to conduct an investigation into someone known in criminal circles as The Prince of Torts. He's only got a name, it seems, behind the illegal activities. Nobody knows who he is.

"During my investigation, C.G. Baneskka is believed to be poisoned—"

"Only he wasn't poisoned," Kendra interrupted. "I saw so myself. He was drugged to make it *look* like he was poisoned, but the drug

wouldn't have killed him."

"Yes, as I was about to say," Cicero

continued. "Sepia told me. Mr. Baneskka was

drugged to take him out of commission long enough

to steal the keys to his mag-lifted trailers and bust

through Renaissance's front gate.

"Some thirty men pile out of the trailers,

charge the barony, wreaking havoc as they go, to get

to a point where they can release a device. All in the

name of some new player called Gauntlet.

"At The Temple at roughly the same time,

not half that many men come out of hiding and

attack attendants of the coronation, but they are

doing so in the name of The Prince of Torts.

"All of this coincides with an accident at a dig site—"

"It wasn't an accident!" Wade shouted above their conspiratorial whispering. He caught himself before continuing. "Nobody believes me, but Cray, Stev, and Kinari were up to something before the explosion."

"She's called you here because she *does* believe you!" Sepia said, sighing deeply. "Will both of you just listen?"

Everyone stayed silent for nearly a minute before Cicero continued.

"Here's what I think happened: The Prince of Torts planned an attack on the coronation with an unknown objective, completely unknowing that

Gauntlet had sent troops to release an unknown

device in Renaissance on the same day."

"That's a lot of unknowns for one sentence,"

Wade said.

"And we *still* don't know what the thing

did," Sepia added. "Once Uncle Wayland cleared

the old hospital, all that was in the room where

Cicero saw the man explode was a black box. A

week of testing. Scanners pick up nothing on it."

"So Cray, Stev, and Kinari rig an explosion

to let Gautlet's crew in," Wade said.

"Kinari was killed in the explosion," Kendra

added.

"Okay, so maybe she doesn't know the plan

and is killed," Wade said. "Regardless, Gauntlet's

guys, they can't just come into The Kingdom easy

as you please, armed as they were. They sneak in

through a tunnel made by the azure serpent they

tortured."

Cicero wondered quietly how Wade jumped

to the conclusion of secret azure serpent tunnels—

her investigation discovered the creature's body

used as cover for the explosion but nothing about

tunnels—but stayed silent.

"But why not kill C.G. with actual poison?"

Kendra interjected. "They clearly weren't above

bloodshed. Why the ruse?"

"What if C.G. was drugged as part of the

Prince's plan?" Sepia jumped in. "Baroness Bedard

only had half the number of balancers on duty she

had expected to because the others were

investigating Mr. Banesska's attack."

"So, the Prince wants Banesska incapacitated but not killed. He just needs a distracted balancer force." Wade says, standing.

"There were only maybe a dozen of The Prince's men at the coronation," Kenrda said, also standing. "Half the working balancers that day would have wiped the floor with them. But then the attack on Renaissance happens."

"And then the dig site explosion!" Wade shouted. Sepia pulled him back down to his seat to shush him.

"Which left no balancers on hand for The Prince's attack," Kendra concluded. She sat back down as well.

"Wait," Kendra said. "We caught that guy! The one guy that we left at the clinic. Have you talked to him?"

"I headed there right after we got things handled that day in Renaissance to do just that," Cicero said. "He had escaped."

"Escaped," Wade half-yelled but caught himself, turning it into a whisper. "How?"

"I don't know," Cicero said. "But I did find him the next day. Or, what was left of him."

"Dead?" Kendra asked.

Cicero nodded, adding, "But Baroness Bedard had already told me not to prioritize The Prince any longer. That Gauntlet was the bigger threat."

"You don't think Baroness Bedard?" Wade

said, his head tilted doubtfully.

Cicero only looked at him, her face blank.

"No!" Sepia said, her eyes wide. "I can't

believe it."

"Magena Bedard and C.G. Banesska are old

friends," Kendra said, shaking her head. "But do

you really think so?"

Cicero was quiet for a long while. Finally,

she said, "I don't know. And because I don't know, I

can't trust Baroness Bedard. And, if I can't trust her,

I can't trust The Quorum or any other leader in The

Kingdom. In turn, this casts doubt on every

organization *within* The Kingdom, potentially even

my own."

"The Bard Guild?" Sepia asked. "You think it goes that far?"

"I don't know," Cicero said. Her eyes fell to the table. "That's the problem."

The table remained silent, each person lost in their own thoughts. Finally, Sepia spoke first.

"So, what's the plan?"

"Yeah," Wade said. "What do you need from us?"

Kendra looked to Cicero then, too, her eyes ready for anything.

It was the look in their eyes that gave Cicero pause. This was a dangerous game she meant to play. The kind played for keeps, where the losers don't go home afterward.

But she had no other option.

"Each of you has ties to key parts of The Kingdom, between the Digger and Technolomist guilds, and Sepia, your uncle is a member of The Quorum."

As the hours rolled on, a plan formed. A mission. Finally, instructions given and orders relayed, the four people made to leave before the inn opened properly.

"Before you all go," Cicero said. "I know I don't need to further stress that you can't tell *anyone* about *any* of this."

"We know," Sepia said. "And we won't. We're The Knights Astray. We're good at secrets."

"The Knights Astray," Kendra said, putting her hand out.

"The Knights Astray," Wade smiled, putting

his hand on Kendra's.

Cicero didn't understand whatever the inside

joke was.

"I mean," Sepia said, putting her hand on

Wade's. "If you don't know if there's anyone else

you can stand with, stand with us."

Cicero waited for a beat. Then two more.

Finally, she put her hand on Sepia's.

"The Knights Astray."

Explore more of the world of Harrowed

Earth in Book Three of the ongoing series, *Sordid*

Deals!

www.ingramcontent.com/pod-product-compliance
Lightning Source LLC
Chambersburg PA
CBHW050742230626
47052CB00004BA/1069